Crocs and Rocks

Written by Teresa Heapy

Collins

Kakadu Park

Kakadu is a huge park!

Kakadu Park has beaches and gorges.

gorge

4

It also has cliffs, woods, forests, rivers, mudflats and swamps.

mudflats

swamp

Getting around

Kakadu Park is gigantic! It would take ages to walk around it.

Most visitors come by car or bus.

Noisy foxes

Flying foxes call to each other constantly. They roost in large, noisy groups in rainforests and swamps.

9

Secret turtles

Flatback turtles only lay their eggs on a few beaches. One of these is near Kakadu.

People camp here to study the turtles.

Only a few people camp here at a time!

Croc spot!

There are crocodiles all over the park.

Crocodiles open their mouths to release heat.
These reptiles can't sweat to cool down.

A crocodile uses its thrashing tail to lunge!

It takes its prey by surprise.

Fantastic birds

Egret

You can see egrets on a pond called the Anbangbang Billabong. Egrets catch fish by stabbing them with their bills.

I'm bird-watching

Blue-winged kookaburra

bright feathers

A family of kookaburras can nest in the same tree for up to 15 years!

Rock art

But it's not just animals that live in Kakadu. It's been home to people for over 65,000 years.

a painting of a ship

Look at this amazing rock art.

Some of the paintings are 20,000 years old!

This strange painting shows a fish! It's like an X-ray!

19

Originally, clay was used to make paint.

Look at my photos!

flying foxes

flatback turtles

crocodile

birds

paintings

23

 After reading

Letters and Sounds: Phase 5

Word count: 285

Focus phonemes: /ee/ e, y, e-e /j/ g, ge /f/ ph /l/ le /z/ se /igh/ y /w/ wh /ai/ a /ch/ tch /v/ ve /s/ se

Common exception words: of, to, the, are, one, their, people

Curriculum links: Science: Animals, including humans

National Curriculum learning objectives: Reading/word reading: apply phonic knowledge and skills as the route to decode words, read other words of more than one syllable that contain taught GPCs; Reading/comprehension: drawing on what they already know or on background information and vocabulary provided by the teacher

Developing fluency

- Your child may enjoy hearing you read the book.
- Take turns to read a page of text, using different speaking voices for the speech bubbles.

Phonic practice

- Look together at **constantly** on page 8. Challenge your child to separate the syllables as they sound out the word. (*con-stant-ly*)
- Challenge your child to sound out these words in the same way too:

  gi-gan-tic   com-plete-ly   Bill-a-bong

  o-rig-in-all-y   An-bang-bang

Extending vocabulary

- Ask your child to add an -ly ending to these words and read them correctly:

  bright (*brightly*)   live (*lively*)

  strange (*strangely*)   constant (*constantly*)
- Can they use these words in a new, made-up sentence?

Comprehension

- Explain to your child that this book is about Kakadu National Park in Australia. The beautiful rock art on pages 18 to 21 was made by First Nations Australians, who have lived in the area for many thousands of years. The oldest paintings at Kakadu are around 20,000 years old, but painting is still a very important part of First Nations Australians' culture and life.
- Turn to pages 22 and 23 and encourage your child to talk through the photos, explaining what they have learnt about each.